# Jacko

## Pat Thomson
## and Caroline Crossland

**Young Lions**

First published in hardback by
A & C Black (Publishers) Limited
Published in Young Lions 1989
10 9 8 7 6 5

Young Lions is an imprint of
the Children's Division, part of
HarperCollins Publishers Ltd,
77–85 Fulham Palace Road, London W6 8JB

Printed and bound in Great Britain by
HarperCollins Manufacturing Glasgow

## School Gate

Dan stopped at the school gate and turned round. He looked up the street. No one there. He looked down the street. Still no one there. Who had shouted?

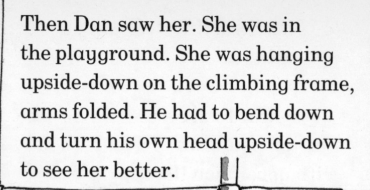

Then Dan saw her. She was in the playground. She was hanging upside-down on the climbing frame, arms folded. He had to bend down and turn his own head upside-down to see her better.

'I'm Dan,' he answered. 'Who are you?'

'Jacko,' said the girl, hanging from first one arm and then the other. She was making chattering chimp noises. 'Where do you live?'

You look like a monkey.

Don't be cheeky.

'49 Fish Street. We've only just moved here.'

'I live near Fish Street,' said Jacko. She jumped down. 'I'll walk home with you, if you like.'

Dan was pleased. There were lots of streets and he was still afraid of getting lost.

5

'I've lived here for years,' said Jacko as they walked along. 'I was born here. In fact, my gran was born here, my dad was born here – even the dog was born here.'

'What's it like?' asked Dan.

'Not bad. A bit dull, I suppose.

'You can swim in the swimming pool.

'You can roller-skate
at the rink.

'You can play
in the park.

'You can fall
in the canal.

7

'That's the only interesting thing, but my mum's not too keen.' Jacko smiled suddenly. 'There's one thing around here that's not boring. It's my family . . . Shall I tell you about them?'

OK – I'm listening.

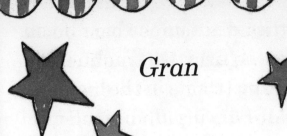

# *Gran*

Dan and Jacko walked slowly down the street. Jacko began to talk.

'Everyone knows my gran,' said Jacko. 'She's well-known round here. She works in the circus.'

'Your gran?' Dan was surprised. 'Does she sell tickets and things?'

'She used to,' said Jacko, 'before it all happened.'

'Before all *what* happened?' said Dan.

Well, they'd put up the big tent on the playing field. One night, Gran was selling tickets in the box office, when Mr Parkinson, the ring master, rushed in with dreadful news.

Everyone felt awful. They were all covered in spots.

'Even the leopards?' asked Dan.

'They were already covered in spots,' said Jacko sternly.

Anyway, it was only the people who had chicken pox. My gran looked at them and took charge immediately. The band was rather itchy but not too spotty, so she told them to play some music. 'I'll be back in a minute,' she said.

When Gran came back, she was riding a beautiful white horse.

She didn't even hold on. She rode once round the ring sitting down. Then she rode standing up—on one leg.

She's used to horses, of course.
The lions were harder.

'The lions?' said Dan. 'She never worked with lions, did she?'

Jacko nodded.

She brought them on and they roared and roared. They didn't know her, you see.

. . . And the biggest lion opened
its mouth. Guess what Gran
did then.

'Put her head in its mouth?'

'Don't be silly – that would have been dangerous.'

No, she gave him a chocolate drop. After that, the lions were like kittens. They held a hoop while Gran jumped through.

Gran thought it would be nice to walk the tightrope. She climbed the ladder, stepped out on to the wire, and wobbled.

'Ooh,' gasped the crowd.

'Oo-er,' gasped Gran. But she made
it to the other side.

Then she swung on the trapeze,
which wasn't so hard. She does that
on our swing.

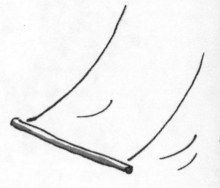

Ooh

Ooh

Ooh

To finish, Gran wanted to be a clown. She likes making people laugh. She put on baggy trousers and a funny hat, and threw buckets of water.

Clowns use little bits of paper, not real water.

Gran didn't know that.

But she put things right by asking
the elephant to give a blow-dry
to anyone who needed it.

When it was all over, the ring master thanked Gran again and again.

Think nothing of it, Mr Parkinson. I'll do it again tomorrow.

# Our Baby

Dan and Jacko stopped for a rest.
There was a low wall in front of
the fish and chip shop. They sat down
and sniffed.

'Our baby eats fish and chips,'
said Jacko.

'Your baby? I thought babies had
milk and soft stuff,' said Dan.

'Not ours. Our baby's different.
She's little but strong. The first
week after Mum brought her home
from hospital, she slept. She looked
lovely, tucked up snugly in her cot.
It all started happening
the second week.

'It was little things at first. She sat up when she was two weeks old. She crawled when she was three weeks. She was singing pop songs when she was four weeks.'

Then she climbed out of her high
chair all alone. She used the bath
like a swimming pool. She liked to
high dive off the towel rail. We
didn't mind. It was good fun.

If we had to move the wardrobe,
we got the baby to help.
But we didn't tell anyone else.

Then one day we ran into trouble.

Mum went up to the baby's room
and the cot was empty. The bars
were bent and the baby was gone.

'My baby! What's happened to her?'
cried Mum.

Baby
bored.

Mum sent for the doctor,
then fainted.

The doctor came, and revived Mum.
He said the baby was all right, but
Mum needed a rest. He bent down
and looked at the cot.

The baby gave him a push and bent
the bars back, trapping his head.
Mum sent for the police,
then fainted.

Brake

Screech

Soon the garden was full of people,
all looking up at the window.

The policemen revived Mum. Then
they put their hands through the
cot bars. 'No baby could bend these,'
they said.

The baby jumped up and bent the bars
round their wrists. Mum sent for
the fire brigade, then fainted.

The crowd went wild when the
fire brigade arrived. The firemen
rushed upstairs. First they revived
Mum (but when she thought of the
newspaper headlines,
she fainted
again).

**Daily Fibber**

**SUPER KID IN ESCAPE BID!**

Attempts to keep Fish Street's Little Wonder out of the public eye failed yesterday. Our little Superstar battled with doctors, the police force and the fire engines of 6 counties, to gain her freedom. What the DAILY FIBBER says is, "Let her go!" The country needs more babies like this.

**Superbaby Loose?**

Full story on Sports Page, next to the crossword. Phone in if you can't find it.

Then they freed the doctor and the policemen. Then they said, 'Where's the baby?' They heard a great cheer from the crowd, and rushed to the window. The baby was climbing down the drainpipe.

Dad had just got home, so he brought her in. 'Want tea now,' she said. So we all had egg with

bread fingers to dip in.

# Dad

'If you saw my dad,' said Jacko,
'you'd think he was quite ordinary.
He's just ordinary with me.

'He's just ordinary with Mum.

'He's as ordinary with Gran as
he can be.

'He's just an ordinary dad, except when he's inventing.'

'Is your dad an inventor, then?' asked Dan.

'Afraid so,' admitted Jacko. 'The first thing he invented was a helpful robot. It was a nice little thing.'

Set the dial on 1,
and the robot
cooks the breakfast.

Set the dial on 2,
and it does
the washing.

Set the dial on 3,
and it hoovers
the carpet.

Set the dial on 4,
and it does
the gardening.

'Sounds great to me,' said Dan.

'Yes,' said Jacko, 'but Dad got the wires crossed. The first time we used it, things went a bit wrong.'

It put the breakfast in the washing machine.

It hoovered the garden.

It put our
dirty clothes
in the oven.

It planted a lovely
bed of flowers
on the carpet.

'Dad also improves things,' Jacko
went on sadly. 'He thought our
vacuum-cleaner wasn't powerful
enough, so he improved that.'

I had a good bicycle once.
Dad thought it would be better as
a flycycle.

He had a go at the baby's high chair.
And now it goes up and down like
a dentist's chair.

Gran has a shopping basket
on wheels. Dad fitted an engine.

Mum's knitting machine used to
be ordinary. Now it knits very
strange things.

'I wish we had an inventor in the family,' said Dan.

'It may sound all right,' said Jacko, 'but you should try living with one. Come on, not far to go now.'

# The Dog

Dan and Jacko turned the corner
and stopped in front of the pet shop.

'Look at that rabbit!' said Jacko.
'Its ears are so long, you could
tie them in a bow.'

'I like the hamster best,' said Dan.
'Look at his little fat cheeks.'

'I bet the parrot can't say anything
except "Pretty Polly",' he added.
'They never can.'

'I'd like to have a kitten,' said Jacko,
'but my mum says a dog's more than
enough trouble.'

Less trouble than
some children, I can
tell you.

'You've got a dog, then?'

'Oh yes,' said Jacko, beginning to walk on again. 'At least, we tell everyone he's a dog. We don't want to worry them.'

'What do you mean?'

'I mean,' said Jacko slowly, 'he's really a wolf.'

'A wolf?' gasped Dan. 'But where did you get him?'

'Probably escaped from the zoo,'
said Jacko quickly.

'All I know is that he limped into
our garden one day, with a thorn
in his paw. He looked so sad, that
I plucked up my courage and took
the thorn out for him. He's been
with us ever since.'

'Is he tame, then?' asked Dan.

'Oh no, not at all. He doesn't like people coming into the garden – that's the problem. The dustbins are never emptied.'

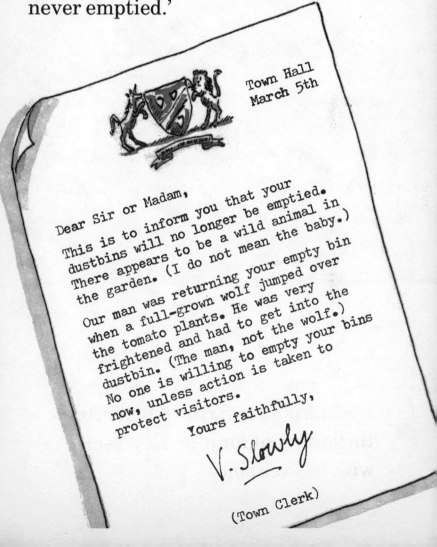

Town Hall
March 5th

Dear Sir or Madam,

This is to inform you that your dustbins will no longer be emptied. There appears to be a wild animal in the garden. (I do not mean the baby.)

Our man was returning your empty bin when a full-grown wolf jumped over the tomato plants. He was very frightened and had to get into the dustbin. (The man, not the wolf.)

No one is willing to empty your bins now, unless action is taken to protect visitors.

Yours faithfully,

V. Slowly

(Town Clerk)

The postmen are very good,
though.

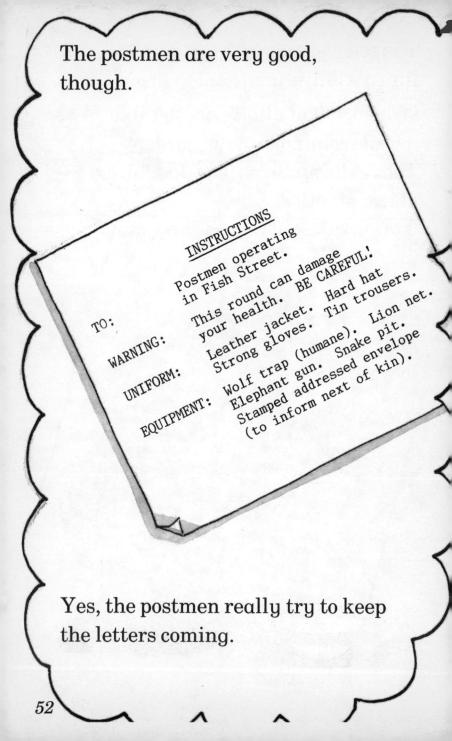

INSTRUCTIONS

Postmen operating
in Fish Street.

TO:

WARNING:     This round can damage
             your health.  BE CAREFUL!

UNIFORM:     Leather jacket.  Hard hat
             Strong gloves.  Tin trousers.

EQUIPMENT:   Wolf trap (humane).  Lion net.
             Elephant gun.  Snake pit.
             Stamped addressed envelope
             (to inform next of kin).

Yes, the postmen really try to keep
the letters coming.

The television people are going to film a wildlife programme in our garden soon.

'Fantastic!' said Dan. 'I can't wait to get to your house.'

Jacko looked at Dan and Dan looked at Jacko, and Jacko began to walk more slowly.

# Jacko's Gate

'Well, here's the top of Fish Street,' said Jacko. 'Can you find your way from here?'

'Yes, thanks,' said Dan, 'but I'd like to meet your family.'

Jacko stopped and did some handstands against the wall. She didn't seem too keen.

'You know my gran?' she said suddenly. 'She sells tickets at the ABC Cinema. She's good with animals, though. She likes cats. She doesn't exactly ride horses, but she once had a ride on a donkey, at the sea-side.'

'And the circus band?' asked Dan.

'The band on the sea front,' said Jacko.

Dan nodded.

'Did I mention our baby?' said Jacko. She was staring down the road, not looking at Dan. 'She's very strong. Well, strong for her age. When Mum gives her some dinner, she bites the spoon and won't let go. Mum says we'll lose the spoon one day.'

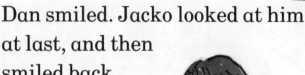

Dan smiled. Jacko looked at him at last, and then smiled back.

'Dad is a sort of inventor,' she said.
'He's making me a go-cart for my
birthday. You can have a ride
if you like.'

'Great,' said Dan. 'You can have a
go on my bike.'

Suddenly, there was a loud barking.
A dog shot out of a gate. It began
speeding towards them like a rocket.

A middle-sized dog, with a brownish
coat, crashed into them.

'He looks just like a wolf, doesn't he?'
said Jacko. 'There's quite a lot of
alsatian in him, anyway.'

Wolf jumped up at Dan. Dan sat
down suddenly – and Wolf began to
lick his face.

'Well,' said Dan, 'I can see why the
dustbin men don't fancy coming
into your garden.'

Dan looked at Jacko's house.
It looked just like his own. If all
those stories were true, there ought
to be special notices up on the wall.

GRAN
Famous Star
of the Circus
lived here

He saw a lady in the garden,
swinging gently on the swing.

SUPERBABY
The Strongest Baby in the World lived here

Dan saw a jolly little baby, sitting on the grass, playing with a toy fire engine.

**SIR GEORGE JACKSON**
○ World Famous ○
Inventor
lived here

A kind-looking man smiled at them
as he tried to mend the gate.
He didn't seem very good at it.

'Your family isn't boring, you know,' said Dan. 'It's got you in it. You must be the best story-teller in the whole world. I nearly believed you.'

Jacko looked pleased. 'I'll tell you some more if you like.'

'Let's walk home together tomorrow, then,' said Dan.